Amelia Bedelia

An I Can Read
Picture Book™

Amelia Bedelia

by **Peggy Parish**

Pictures by Fritz Siebel

HarperFestival®

A Division of HarperCollinsPublishers

HarperCollins®, ☖®, HarperFestival®, and An I Can Read Picture Book ™
are trademarks of HarperCollins Publishers Inc.

Amelia Bedelia
Text copyright © 1963, renewed 1991, by the Estate of Margaret Parish
Illustrations copyright © 1963, renewed 1991, by the Estate of Fritz Siebel
Manufactured in China. All rights reserved.
http://www.harperchildrens.com

Library of Congress Cataloging-in-Publication Data
Parish, Peggy.
  Amelia Bedelia / by Peggy Parish ; pictures by Fritz Siebel.
    p.   cm. — (An I can read picture book)
  Summary: A literal-minded housekeeper causes chaos in the Rogers household
when she attempts to make sense of some instructions.
  ISBN 0-694-01296-3
  [1. Household employees—Fiction.   2. Humorous stories.]   I. Siebel, Fritz, ill.
II. Title.   III. Series.
[PZ7.P219Am   1999]   98-31782
[E]—dc21   CIP
                                                                                  AC

Typography by Tom Starace and David Horowitz
6   7   8   9   10
❖
First An I Can Read Picture Book edition, 1999

For Debbie, John Grier,

Walter, and Michael Dinkins

"Oh, Amelia Bedelia, your first day of work, and I can't be here. But I made a list for you. You do just what the list says," said Mrs. Rogers.

Mrs. Rogers got into the car with Mr. Rogers. They drove away.

"My, what nice folks. I'm going to like working here," said Amelia Bedelia.

Amelia Bedelia went inside. "Such a grand house. These must be rich folks. But I must get to work. Here I stand just looking. And me with a whole list of things to do."

Amelia Bedelia stood there a minute longer. "I think I'll make a surprise for them. I'll make lemon-meringue pie. I do make good pies."

So Amelia Bedelia went into the kitchen. She put a little of this and a pinch of that into a bowl. She mixed and she rolled.

Soon her pie was ready to go into the oven.

"There," said Amelia Bedelia. "That's done."

"Now let's see what this list says."

Amelia Bedelia read,

Change the towels in the green bathroom.

Amelia Bedelia found the green bathroom.

"Those towels are very nice. Why change them?"

she thought.

Then Amelia Bedelia remembered what Mrs. Rogers had said. She must do just what the list told her. "Well, all right," said Amelia Bedelia.

Amelia Bedelia got some scissors. She snipped a little here and a little there. And she changed those towels.

"There," said Amelia Bedelia.

She looked at her list again.

Dust the furniture.

"Did you ever hear tell of such a silly thing. At my house we undust the furniture. But to each his own way."

Amelia Bedelia took one last look at the bathroom. She saw a big box with the words *Dusting Powder* on it.

"Well, look at that. A special powder to dust with!" exclaimed Amelia Bedelia. So Amelia Bedelia dusted the furniture.

"That should be dusty enough. My, how nice it smells."

Draw the drapes when the sun comes in.

read Amelia Bedelia.

She looked up. The sun was coming in. Amelia Bedelia looked at the list again.

"Draw the drapes? That's what it says. I'm not much of a hand at drawing, but I'll try."

So Amelia Bedelia sat right down and she drew those drapes.

Amelia Bedelia marked off about the

drapes. "Now what?"

*Put the lights out when you
finish in the living room.*

Amelia Bedelia thought about this a minute.
She switched off the lights. Then she carefully
unscrewed each bulb.

And Amelia Bedelia put the lights out.

"So those things need to be aired out, too.

Just like pillows and babies. Oh, I do have a lot to

learn."

"My pie!" exclaimed Amelia Bedelia. She hurried to the kitchen.

"Just right," she said. She took the pie out of
the oven and put it on the table to cool. Then she
looked at the list.

Measure two cups of rice.

"That's next," said Amelia Bedelia. Amelia
Bedelia found two cups. She filled them with rice.

And Amelia Bedelia measured
that rice.

Amelia Bedelia laughed. "These folks do want me to do funny things."

Then she poured the rice back into the container.

The meat market will deliver
a steak and a chicken.

Please trim the fat before you
put the steak in the icebox.

And please dress the chicken.

When the meat arrived, Amelia Bedelia
opened the bag. She looked at the steak
for a long time. "Yes," she said. "That
will do nicely."

Amelia Bedelia got some lace and bits of ribbon. And Amelia Bedelia trimmed that fat before she put the steak in the icebox.

"Now I must dress the chicken. I wonder if she wants a he chicken or a she chicken?" said Amelia Bedelia.

Amelia Bedelia went right to work. Soon the chicken was finished.

Amelia Bedelia heard the door open. "The folks are back," she said. She rushed out to meet them.

"Amelia Bedelia, why are all the light bulbs outside?" asked Mr. Rogers.

"The list just said to put the lights out," said
Amelia Bedelia. "It didn't say to bring them back
in. Oh, I do hope they didn't get aired too long."

"Amelia Bedelia, the sun will fade the furniture. I asked you to draw the drapes," said Mrs. Rogers.

"I did! I did! See," said Amelia Bedelia. She held up her picture.

Then Mrs. Rogers saw the furniture.

"The furniture!" she cried.

"Did I dust it well enough?" asked
Amelia Bedelia. "That's such nice
dusting powder."

Mr. Rogers went to wash his hands.

"I say," he called. "These are very unusual

towels."

Mrs. Rogers dashed into the bathroom. "Oh, my best towels," she said.

"Didn't I change them enough?" asked Amelia Bedelia.

Mrs. Rogers went to the kitchen. "I'll cook the dinner. Where is the rice I asked you to measure?"

"I put it back in the container. But I
remember—it measured four and a half inches,"
said Amelia Bedelia.

"Was the meat delivered?" asked Mrs. Rogers.

"Yes," said Amelia Bedelia. "I trimmed the fat just like you said. It does look nice."

Mrs. Rogers rushed to the icebox. She opened it. "Lace! Ribbons! Oh, dear!" said Mrs. Rogers.

"The chicken—you dressed the chicken?" asked Mrs. Rogers.

"Yes, and I found the nicest box to put him in," said Amelia Bedelia.

"Box!" exclaimed Mrs. Rogers.

Mrs. Rogers hurried over to the box. She lifted the lid. There lay the chicken. And he was just as dressed as he could be.

Mrs. Rogers was angry. She was very angry. She opened her mouth.

Mrs. Rogers meant to tell Amelia Bedelia she was fired. But before she could get the words out, Mr. Rogers put something in her mouth. It was so good Mrs. Rogers forgot about being angry.

"Lemon-meringue pie!" she exclaimed.

"I made it to surprise you," said Amelia Bedelia happily.

So right then and there Mr. and Mrs. Rogers decided that Amelia Bedelia must stay.

And so she did.

Mrs. Rogers learned to say undust the furniture, unlight the lights, close the drapes, and things like that.

Mr. Rogers didn't care if Amelia Bedelia

trimmed all of his steaks with lace.

All he cared about was having her there

to make lemon-meringue pie.